A DORLING KINDERSLEY BOOK

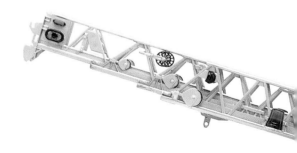

Photography by Stephen Oliver
Illustrations by Jane Cradock–Watson
and Dave Hopkins
**Truck consultant and models
supplied by** Ted Taylor

Copyright © 1991 by Dorling Kindersley Limited, London

LITTLE SIMON MERCHANDISE
An imprint of Simon & Schuster
Children's Publishing Division
1230 Avenue of the Americas
New York, New York 10020

Eye Openers™

First published in Great Britain in 1991
by Dorling Kindersley Limited,
9 Henrietta Street, London WC2E 8PS

Reproduced by Colourscan, Singapore
Printed and bound in Italy by L.E.G.O., Vicenza

7 8 9 10

ISBN 0-689-71405-X

Library of Congress CIP data is available.

·EYE·OPENERS·
Trucks

LITTLE SIMON

Delivery truck

Delivery trucks make short trips. They deliver goods to stores. The back of the truck rolls up for easy unloading.

cab

TURBO INTERCOOLING 2800

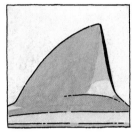

light   air deflector

Snowplow

In winter, a snowplow is used to clear snow from the roads. The large plow blade pushes the snow into big piles. The dumper at the back carries sand. The back tips up and scatters sand on to the icy road.

plow blade

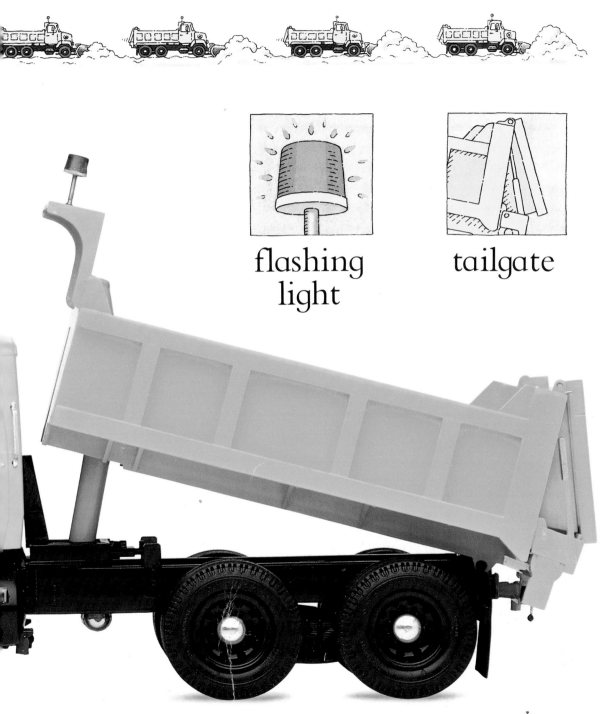

flashing
light

tailgate

9

Cement mixer

This truck delivers cement to building sites. The cement is made in the big mixing drum. The drum turns round and round. The cement pours out down the trough at the back.

hood

mixing
drum

trough

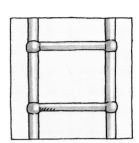

ladder

mud-flap

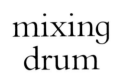 11

Fire engine

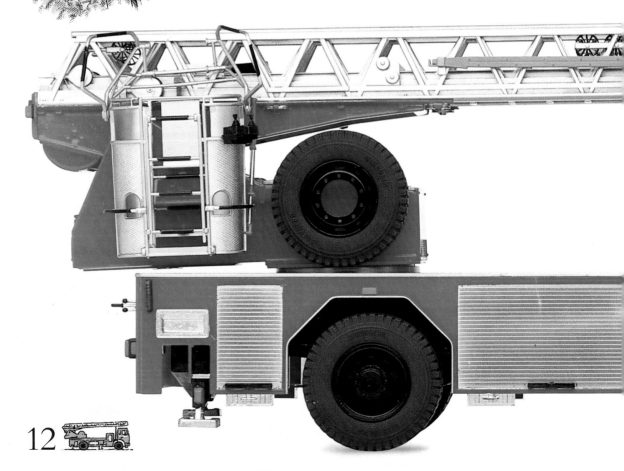

A fire engine has a long ladder. It reaches to the top of tall buildings. The fireman climbs up the ladder and stands in the cage. He rescues people from smoke and flames.

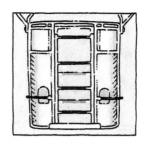

flashing light   cage   water hose

ladder

SDF 304

F613

Crane

Cranes are used to lift heavy loads like concrete slabs or bricks. They can unload materials at building sites quickly and easily. The legs at the back hold the truck steady.

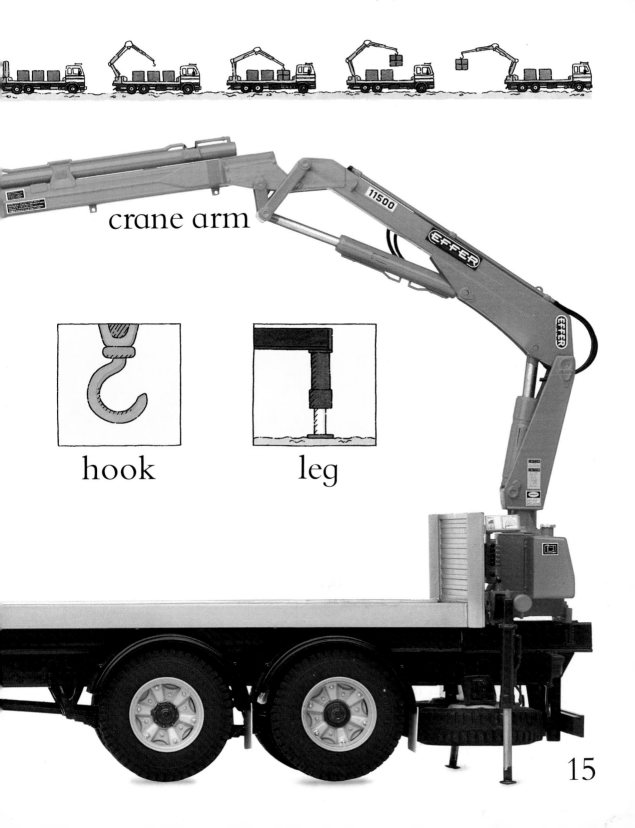

crane arm

hook

leg

15

Tanker

Trucks called tankers are used to transport gasoline. Gasoline is carried in the big tank at the back. At the gas station the gasoline is pumped down a hose into underground tanks.

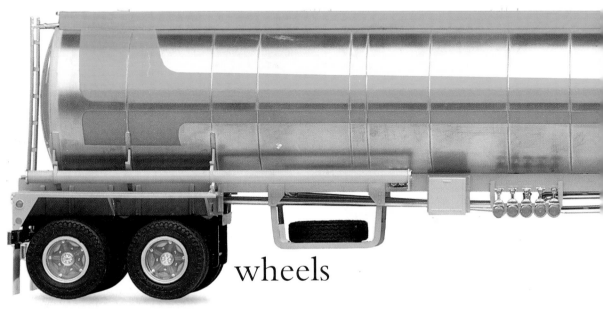

wheels

hose

rearview
mirror

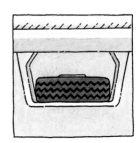

spare
wheel

tank

air
deflector

Tow truck

A tow truck rescues
cars that have broken
down or had an
accident. The car
is hooked on to the
crane at the back.
The truck tows the
car to a garage
for repairs.

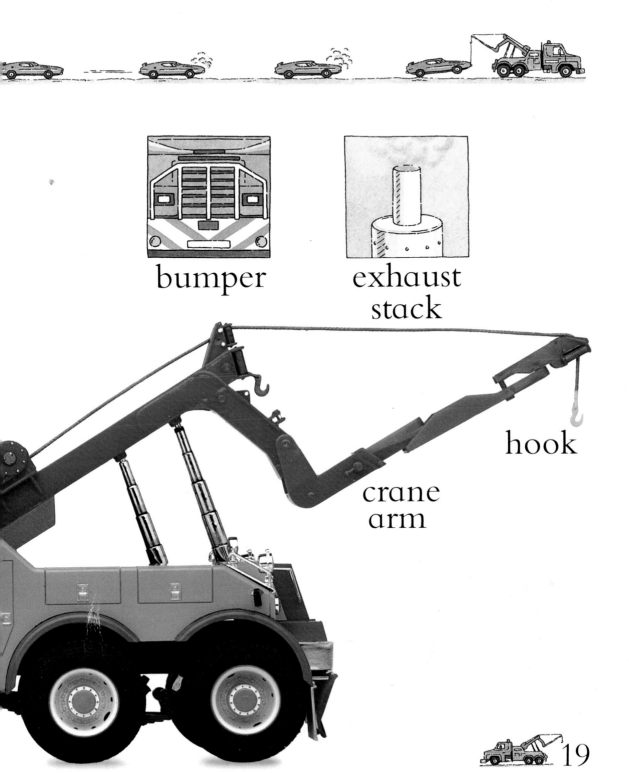

bumper

exhaust
stack

hook

crane
arm

19

Car transporter

Car transporters deliver cars from the factory. The cars can be driven on and off using the ramp. The cab of this truck tips forward, so that the mechanic can work on the engine.

tipper
cab

engine

ramp

trailer